Yellow-Eye

Tapatjatjaka Community Government Council of Titjikala, Northern Territory, Australia, endorses this story as a positive and worthwhile contribution towards intercultural understanding and reconciliation.

To the many indigenous people who have offered their friendship and the gifts of wisdom, especially to Scott Gorringe, Lincoln Boko and the wonderful people of Titjikala.

> D.S.

To my father for his love and inspiration.

> M.W.

Acknowledgements

A. O. Kawagley, and R.Barnhardt, "Education Indigenous to Place: Western Science Meets Native Reality" in *Ecological Education in Action*, edited by G. A. Smith and D. R. Williams (State University of New York Press, 1999).

M. J. Christie, "Aboriginal Science for the Ecologically Sustainable Future" in *NGOONJOOK: Batchelor Journal of Aboriginal Education* (November, 1990).

First American edition published in 2002 by
CROCODILE BOOKS
An imprint of Interlink Publishing Group, Inc.
99 Seventh Avenue, Brooklyn, New York 11215 and
46 Crosby Street, Northampton, Massachusetts 01060

Library of Congress Cataloging-in-Publication Data
Spillman, David, 1961- .
Yellow-eye / written by David Spillman; illustrated by Mark Wilson.--
1st American ed.
     p. c.m.
Summary: When the yellow-fish become scarce, members of the Impatjara community and Australian government officials must learn to work cooperatively to bring the fish back.
ISBN 1-56656-410-7
1. Australian aborigines--Juvenile fiction. [1. Australian aborigines--Fiction. 2. Australia--Fiction.] I. Wilson, Mark, ill. II. Title.
PZ7. S7555 Ye 2001
[Fic]--dc21

                    2001001231

Printed and bound in Hong Kong

10 9 8 7 6 5 4 3 2 1

To request our complete 48-page full-color catalog, please call us at 1-800-238-LINK, visit our website at www.interlinkbooks.com, or write to us at:
Interlink Publishing, 46 Crosby Street, Northampton, MA 01060
E-mail: sales@interlinkbooks.com

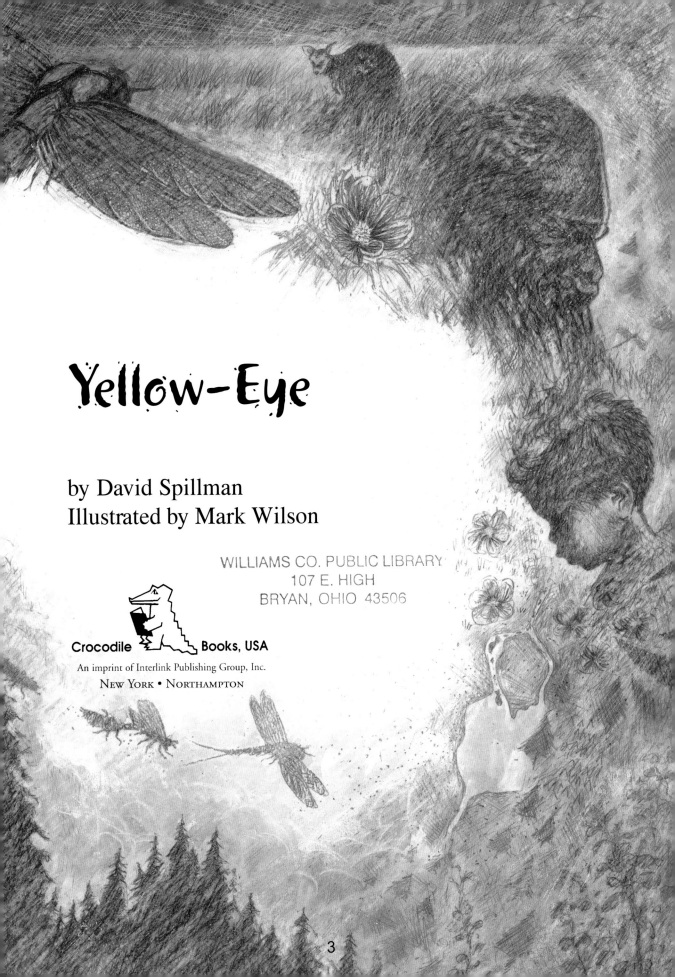

Yellow-Eye

by David Spillman
Illustrated by Mark Wilson

Crocodile Books, USA
An imprint of Interlink Publishing Group, Inc.
NEW YORK • NORTHAMPTON

My grandfather, Ningi, drew a picture of our country in the dirt. He always drew the same picture. All his stories started this way.

"Great River Kanatya, our life source, flowing through this country, our mother. We walk this country, the forests, mountains, and plains. We know her well. Great Spirit Yana makes Yanatji, the beautiful flower, grow here. Yanatji calls up Yellow-eye to lay her eggs. Soon after, we catch many Yellow-eye in the lake. We sing, dance, and tell many stories to show our mother and great Yana we are grateful for Yellow-eye."

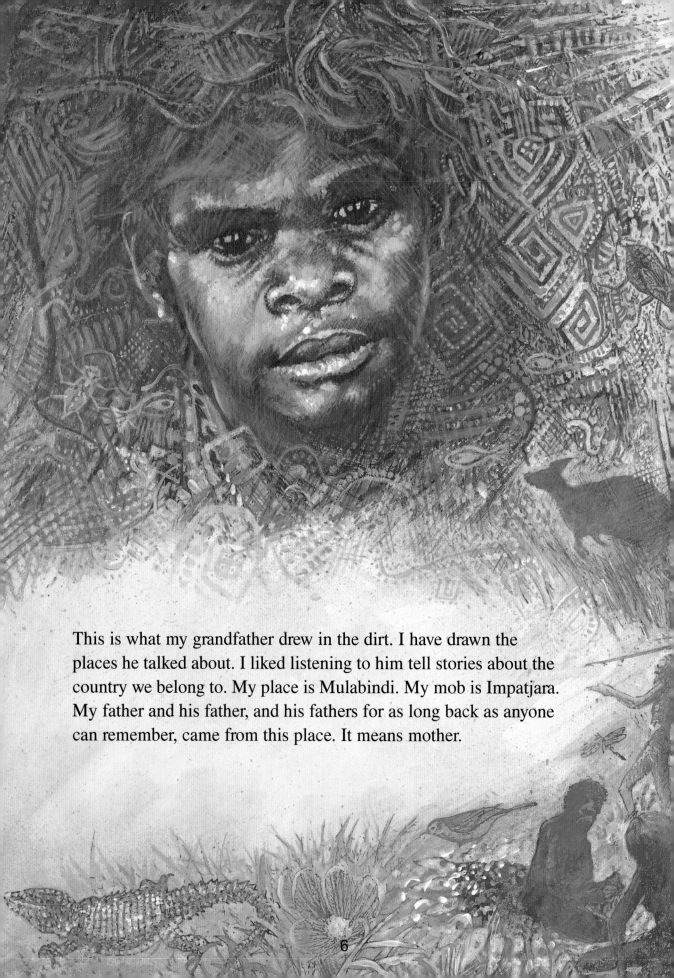

This is what my grandfather drew in the dirt. I have drawn the places he talked about. I liked listening to him tell stories about the country we belong to. My place is Mulabindi. My mob is Impatjara. My father and his father, and his fathers for as long back as anyone can remember, came from this place. It means mother.

I want to tell you a story that happened when I was about twelve. It's a wonderful story, but it makes me sad, too.

I was listening to my grandfather when some Newmob drove up in four-wheel drives.

"What are they here for?" I asked my grandfather.
"Meeting," he said, standing up.
"What about, Grandfather?"
"Yellow-eye, I think," he replied. "This mob fish dreaming," he said pointing to the vehicle with a fish painted on its door.

"What's that one?" I asked him, pointing to the other four-wheel drive.
"Don't know. Never see that one," he mumbled, walking off towards
the office.

Now kids didn't usually go to meetings with Newmob at Mulabindi.
Too boring, I guessed. But I thought this meeting would be interesting
since it was about Yellow-eye. I spotted Uncle Ehboy walking towards
the office. He was on the Council, too.

"Great Uncle, can I come? I want to hear about Yellow-eye."
"No talking, boy," he replied. That meant yes.

In the office all the members of the Council were sitting on chairs. Paul, a Newmob man we all knew, sat on the desk in the front. He had come to Mulabindi many times. Another Newmob man I had never seen before, sat on a chair beside him.

After a while Paul stood and began to speak.

"Council of Mulabindi, many of you know me. My name is Paul. I work for the Department of Fisheries. You know I've been counting and measuring Yellow-eye for five years now. You know their numbers are dropping, and they are getting smaller. You, the Council of Mulabindi, have been asking the government to do something about this for a long time."

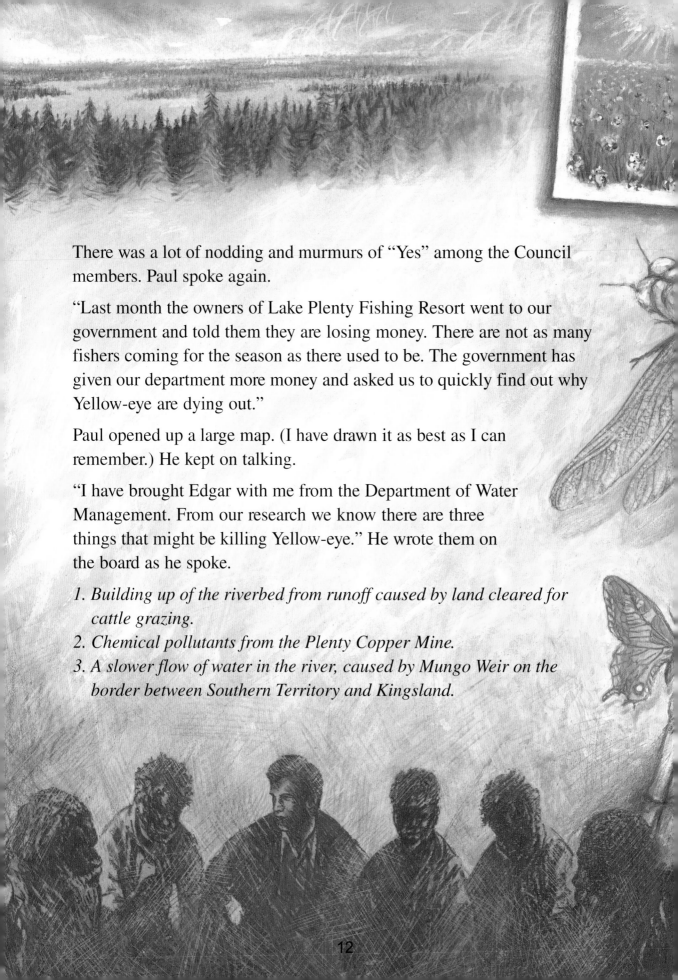

There was a lot of nodding and murmurs of "Yes" among the Council members. Paul spoke again.

"Last month the owners of Lake Plenty Fishing Resort went to our government and told them they are losing money. There are not as many fishers coming for the season as there used to be. The government has given our department more money and asked us to quickly find out why Yellow-eye are dying out."

Paul opened up a large map. (I have drawn it as best as I can remember.) He kept on talking.

"I have brought Edgar with me from the Department of Water Management. From our research we know there are three things that might be killing Yellow-eye." He wrote them on the board as he spoke.

1. *Building up of the riverbed from runoff caused by land cleared for cattle grazing.*
2. *Chemical pollutants from the Plenty Copper Mine.*
3. *A slower flow of water in the river, caused by Mungo Weir on the border between Southern Territory and Kingsland.*

FORESTRY PLANTATION

FORESTRY PLANTATION

KINGSLAND

RIVER KANATYA

MUNGO WEIR

CATTLE GRAZING

CATTLE GRAZING

SOUTHERN TERRITORY

PLENTY

COPPER MINE

LAKE PLENTY FISHING RESORT

LAKE PLENTY

MULABINDI

CATTLE GRAZING

NATURAL FOREST

"Edgar is going to measure the sediment in the river, the level of chemical pollutants, and how fast the water is flowing. He is going to show you the instruments he will use."

Just as Edgar got up to speak, my grandfather stood and asked excitedly, "You see Yanatji?"
Paul and Edgar looked at each other and shrugged. Then Paul looked at my grandfather and said, "What is Yanatji?"

All of a sudden there was a lot of yelling and talking among the Council members. I couldn't hear what they were saying, but it sounded as if they were telling each other off. Paul began waving his hands and calling out, "Quiet down, please." He must have said it ten times. After a while everyone stopped talking. My grandfather sat down and looked at the floor.

Edgar showed the Council his instruments. He said, "If you see these when you are fishing, please leave them alone. They are very expensive and will tell us why Yellow-eye are dying."

At the end of the meeting Paul asked, "Are there any questions?" He then told us that they would come back tomorrow to show us where they were putting the instruments. There was silence. The old people stood and walked out without talking.

Outside I ran to catch up with Uncle Ehboy as he was walking quickly towards the house.

"Uncle Ehboy, what were the old people talking about? What upset them?"

Uncle Ehboy stopped, squatted down, and looked at me.

"Tom, you know that Yanatji brings up Yellow-eye. When Yanatji blooms, Yellow-eye comes within one moon. The old people were saying that if Newmob don't know Yanatji, then they know nothing about Yellow-eye. If Yanatji does not come back, there will be no happy Yellow-eye, no matter how much talking and measuring they do."

"Does Grandfather know where Yanatji has gone?" I asked.

Uncle Ehboy looked at me as if I should know the answer. "Yes, Tom, of course he knows."

"Then you must tell Paul to ask him to speak," I pleaded.

"Tom, Newmob do not ask us questions about such things. They have their own ways of finding things out," Uncle Ehboy replied.

"Then you must tell Grandfather to stand and speak," I offered desperately.

"Tom, you know the old people will not speak to outsiders unless they are asked to."

"Then *you* must speak, Uncle Ehboy. You know where Yanatji has gone."

"Tom, you know I can't speak for the old people. It's not my place. It would be very shameful."

"Then you must make Newmob ask Grandfather. It's for Yellow-eye. That means everything to the old people." By this time I was crying.

Uncle Ehboy stood and looked off towards the river for a while. Then he squatted down again and looked at me. He put his hand on my shoulder. "I think you are right, Tom. I think you are right." He sighed and smiled, then stood up and walked off.

The next day the Council was in the office again.
I was there, too.

Paul stood and began to speak very softly.

"Council of Mulabindi, I'm sorry. I have not acted with respect. I didn't know that the old people have been looking after Yellow-eye for a long time. Nobody told me that. I just thought you fished for Yellow-eye and ate them. But yesterday one of you came and spoke to me. Now I know that the old people have something to say. Ningi, please speak."

Uncle Ehboy looked at me and winked. Grandfather stood, raised his arms and began to speak.

"Since our ancestors walked this land we have been living with Yellow-eye, our brother. Yellow-eye is strong if Yanatji, the beautiful flower, calls him.
"Some time ago Newmob brought cattle to this land. We are glad for cattle. The cattle did not make Yellow-eye sick.

"Newmob built a wall across great River Kanatya, but it did not stop her flowing and giving us life. Mungo Weir did not make Yellow-eye sick.

"Newmob dug a big hole in the ground to take out rocks. Now they give our men work and pay them well. It is not the mine that made Yellow-eye sick.

"Yanatji, the beautiful flower, was happy even after the cattle, the dam, and the mines. You have not seen all this. You have been here for such a short time."

Grandfather turned to face Paul. Now he spoke in a stronger voice.

"It is the forests on the plains that make Yellow-eye sick. The forests stop Yanatji from coming and calling up Yellow-eye. The forests are too dark and noisy. Yanatji needs the sun and to hear great Yana calling. What will you do about the forests?"

Paul looked confused. "You say it is the forests on the plains?" Grandfather nodded. "These forests, are they the ones over the border in Kingsland?" Again Grandfather nodded. "I don't understand how the forests are killing Yellow-eye," Paul said.

"You look and you will see," replied Grandfather.

"Well that will be difficult, Ningi. We'll have to talk with people from the Department of Forestry in Kingsland," Paul said. "We've never done that before. I don't know if they will help."

Grandfather looked at Paul and said again, "Look and you will see."

Paul nodded. "I will try."

The meeting stopped soon after that. We didn't see Paul for a long time. Then one day he rang Uncle Ehboy and told him that they had found out what was killing Yellow-eye. Grandfather was right. Paul asked the Council for permission to write a book about it.

Two years later we read the book at school. It was dedicated to Grandfather. It told how Grandfather's knowledge of Yellow-eye and our country had led the researchers to the cause. We read that:

Yanatji blooms on the plains near the River Kanatya just before the big wet.

Little insects called nizbets feed on the Yanatji nectar. We already knew that.

When Yellow-eye swim up the creeks to lay their eggs, they feed on the nymphs.

Some nymphs survive and grow to shed their skin …

But then it told us something we didn't know. Nizbets lay their eggs in small creeks that flow into the River Kanatya.

The eggs grow into baby nizbets called nymphs.

and become adult nizbets.

Long ago, Yanatji grew on the open plain along the River Kanatya. There was bright sunlight for the grass and flowers to grow.

Then Newmob came and planted pine trees for timber. They planted them everywhere, right down to the water's edge.

When the trees grew, they were so close together that no sunlight could get through, so the grass and the flowers died.

Nizbets did not come to lay their eggs because there was no Yanatji nectar. When Yellow-eye came up the creeks there was no food for them. So they stopped coming. They started laying their eggs near Mungo Weir. But without the right conditions the eggs — and Yellow-eye — were weak.

This story made me see that Impatjara and Newmob work in different ways. We have been here for a long time. We know the seasons. We know how all things relate to each other — plants, animals, people, spirits, and the land. But Newmob look really closely at one little bit at a time.

This story showed me that when we work together with respect we can help each other. We can learn from each other.

Later, the forests were cut down and grass was planted. After a long time Yanatji came back. Now there are plenty of Yellow-eye again. They are happy and strong because Yanatji calls them.

I am a teacher now at Mulabindi School. I decided to become a teacher to teach our children how to talk to Newmob, and how to think and do things their way, as well as Impatjara way.

Uncle Ehboy is an elder now. He is happy. Everyone is happy.
Grandfather did not live to see Yellow-eye return, but his spirit is singing.
I hear him sometimes with the breeze through the trees.